The 420 Uh-Oh

Anne Eton

This paperback is also available as an ebook at most online ebook retailers.

Copyright 2013 Beginnings Press

ISBN-13: 978-1-62602-033-7

ISBN-10: 1626020337

Charlotte Hammarskjold wondered if she should put on her sunglasses. The sun was blazing directly over her, and she was starting to see sunspots through her eyelids.

She considered. Suntanning naked was something she had never tried before. And President Nixon had said something just the other day about skin cancer. Still…she felt that her pasty white skin was completely unsuitable for the hip crowd that Bob seemed to hang with here in San Diego.

Tanning naked had been Bob's idea. "Catch some rays *au naturel* on the deck, babe," he had said before rushing off to yet another one of his urgent meetings. He had given her his wolfish smile. "Nobody will see you. It's Mission Beach. Nobody comes around here. The houses next door are rentals, and it's off-season."

"But what if someone walks down the beach?"

"Never gonna happen. Nobody comes around here. Trust me. Go ahead and tan naked. Then once you're nice and bronzed, we can take some pictures." He had winked.

She had told him emphatically that that would never happen. Then she had tousled his shoulder-length brown hair. But after he had left, she had decided to try tanning naked after all.

Charlotte was, as a rule, shy about her body. Her curvy figure often drew stares, even back in Wisconsin where people bundled up. A friend had once described her body as "luscious." Charlotte didn't think it was all that great. However, men seemed to appreciate her hourglass curves and long blonde hair. She had never enjoyed the attention.

Lying on the redwood deck, Charlotte shut her eyes tighter. She grimaced. Moving her hands behind her head, she tried to make a pillow out of her long blonde hair. The redwood deck was uncomfortable. Why hadn't she brought out a towel? Because she had wanted to go "all natural," that's why. *If you're going to do something, do it all the way. What nonsense!* The suntan lotion on her body was not a natural product, she was sure. She felt it beginning to run off her perspiring skin.

Her eyes began stinging. The suntan lotion had found its way in. Charlotte sighed with exasperation. She sat up like a spring, making her big boobs bounce. As she opened her eyes, she emitted a small scream.

A young woman about her age was standing at the deck's edge, leaning on the railing, watching her.

* * *

Charlotte fumbled, trying to cover herself up.

"No 'hello?'" the stranger asked. Her black hair was buzz-cut, tomboy style, and her plain blue windbreaker and jeans seemed entirely out of place on the beach during a warm day.

"Who the heck are YOU?" Charlotte stood and hurried toward the sliding-glass window.

"'The heck?'"

Charlotte stopped. She turned, flushing. It wasn't easy keeping herself covered with just her hands. "What did you say?"

A slow smile spread over the woman's face. She seemed like someone who did not smile very often. "I said, 'The heck?' As in, did you really just say, 'The heck?'"

"Get out of here. My boyfriend will call the cops."

"No he won't."

"Oh yes he will."

"He left this place over an hour ago."

Charlotte stared. "Who are you, and what do you want?"

"The better question is, who are you?" The woman's eyes traveled, as if reluctantly, up and down Charlotte's glistening nakedness. "I've never seen you before."

"Fine. My boyfriend's not home. I'M calling the cops."

"Good idea. Tell them Regina's here. Ask them to pick up a burger for me on the way."

Charlotte blinked.

"Listen." Regina sighed. "You don't want to get involved with Bob Custis. Trust me."

"What, are you his ex or something?"

At this Regina laughed loud and long.

"What's so funny?"

"Oh God." Regina wiped her eyes. "You know, people tell me I need to laugh more. And that was really funny. Thanks."

"Look…MA'AM." Charlotte shifted uncomfortably. She was standing naked on a beach deck, in a new town, being interrogated by a person who clearly had no manners at all. "If you're the police, I'm sorry about sunbathing without clothes. It wasn't my idea. It'll never happen again."

"Yeah. Well, technically, it's against the law. But you know what? Far as I'm concerned you can tan naked whenever you want, as much as you want." Regina caught herself. She stood up straighter. "Nobody has ever told me I'm a particularly nice person. But right now, I'm trying to do you a favor. You need to get out of Bob's life. I guarantee you won't regret it."

"Yeah?" Charlotte wiped her face, trying to remove some suntan oil from her eyes. Her exposed big boobs wobbled with the movement. She noticed Regina's eyes glance. "Well," Charlotte continued, covering up again, "how would you like it if some chick showed up at your pad and told you to ditch your old man?"

"I think I'd have an even bigger laugh than what I just had. Look…Charlotte. That's your name, right?"

"How did you know?"

"The same way I know this: Bob is involved in some very bad stuff. You seem like a nice kid. I'd hate for you to go down with him."

This made Charlotte angrier than anything else. "Kid? You look my age. Who the heck do you think you are? I want you out of here. I don't care if you're a cop. If you are on this property, you need a warrant, otherwise I will press charges for trespass."

Regina grinned. "My my, legal jargon. You got an attorney?"

"You better believe I'll get one."

"I don't doubt it. I'm leaving. You're welcome, by the way."

The brunette turned and walked away, sashaying in her tight jeans.

Inside, Charlotte threw on some clothes, shaking.

What the heck was that?

Sitting on the bed that she had shared with Bob the night before, she glanced at a stack of boxes that she had not yet unpacked. Her dissertation research. *Who can write a PhD thesis with all these stupid distractions?* she thought.

She had met Bob two weeks ago as she was walking across campus at the University of Wisconsin-Madison. Bob had stopped her to ask where he could find a bite to eat. Soon, they were sharing a meal. And things had progressed from there. Bob had invited her back to San Diego with him.

It was perfect timing. She had just finished her doctoral coursework, and needed to hole up for a while to write her dissertation. She'd offered to ride back with Bob in his Winnebago, but he had demurred. He had a few buddies with him, he had said. Then he had offered to buy her a plane ticket. He seemed rich!

And now, here, on her first full day in San Diego, she'd been accosted by a tough-talking and tough-looking woman who claimed she was a cop, and who was telling her to leave Bob. Saying that Bob was involved in "bad stuff." What did *that* mean?

Charlotte rubbed her temples. It was a lot to process. Her parents had disapproved of her simply packing up and leaving for the West Coast with a man she had known only a few days. She had patiently tried to explain to them that it was, after all, 1972. Her parents had simply shook their heads.

"Is he Norwegian, at least?" her father had asked. Dad was so cute.

Bob had assured Charlotte that she could call her folks any time she wanted. *Don't worry about the long-distance charges,* he had said, *I can cover it.* Charlotte was sure he could. A big house on the beach, lots of wine, the biggest television that she had ever seen—it was all very heady.

Bob had told her he made his money gambling at the track. That's where he was now, actually. Charlotte didn't know what to think about Bob's work, but she supposed that everyone had to make a living. Gambling was legal, after all.

She sighed. Glancing at her skin, she saw some redness. Sunburned already? Maybe it was just as well that that bitchy woman, Regina, had come by. Charlotte rose and walked over Afghan rugs to a bathroom filled with incense candles and cedarwood paneling. Maybe a shower would help her think.

* * *

Two days later, Charlotte was walking over the beautiful polished Spanish tiles that practically paved the hilltop at the University of San Diego. Her brown caftan dress fluttered in the breeze, partially held down by a big shoulder bag. She passed a big fountain in front of the university's mission church and paused to admire the big bell near the apex of the church's front.

She entered the library. After a lengthy conversation with an elderly woman behind the reference desk, Charlotte perused the card catalog before finally sitting down at a small study table next to a sunny window. She withdrew a few papers from her big bag.

"I bet you were the kind of kid who liked homework."

Charlotte looked up. She groaned.

Regina sat across the study table from her, smirking.

"I will press charges against you for harassment," Charlotte said.

"I guess you found a lawyer, then."

"I'm serious. Why are you bothering me?"

Regina leaned her chair back on its rear legs. Her arm draped behind it in a tough-girl pose. It looked natural. "I guess we have a difference of opinion on that point."

Charlotte glared. "Oh, right. You're trying to help me. Thanks so much. Be sure to send me a bill."

"Don't worry about it. I'm a giver."

Turning red, Charlotte leaned forward. "Get this. I'm not kidding. LEAVE ME ALONE."

Regina nodded at the papers in front of Charlotte. "The librarian told me you were looking for books."

"What?"

"The reference librarian. Old lady, glasses, who you talked with about twenty minutes ago? She said you had a list. Something about interlibrary loan."

Charlotte folded her arms. "What business is it

of yours?"

"Hostile. Manners, please. What, do you think I'm going to steal your thesis?"

"Who says I have a thesis?"

"I do." Regina grinned. "I'm smarter than I look. The librarian said you wanted books on Scottish poets. All primary sources. That means you're doing research. And, though some may really enjoy getting into the diary of the neighbor of Robert Burns, it's not exactly leisure reading. So I'm guessing you're writing an English PhD dissertation."

The blonde nodded with grudging respect. "Yeah."

"Also, I happen to have found that out anyway. But I like to think I would've put it all together by myself."

"I'm calling campus security." Charlotte stood up.

"Sit down."

Something in Regina's tone made Charlotte slowly sink back into her seat.

Regina stared into Charlotte's eyes. "For the last time: I'm trying to help you." Pause. "Did you talk to Bob? About me?"

"Why should I tell you?"

Regina waited.

Charlotte sighed. "No. It was too weird. I didn't want him thinking…I dunno. I don't know what I wanted, or didn't want, him to think."

"That's the problem."

"What?"

"That you care about what he thinks. You need to stop caring. Right now."

Charlotte looked out the window. She was trying to appear brave, but she was beginning to feel scared.

"Look," Regina said. "I'm risking my job by telling you this. But I'm going to tell you anyway. Why, God only knows."

"It's hard to feel sorry for someone who won't even tell me what she does, who she is, or—"

"Bob Custis is the biggest 420 smuggler in the United States."

"What do you mean, 420?"

"Marijuana."

The silence lasted over a minute.

"Whaaa…" Charlotte finally began. "How?"

"How? Well, he takes a Winnebago to Mexico, loads it up with bales of weed, then drives it back over the border."

Charlotte said nothing.

"I'm betting you met him up north. He was probably at your campus. Right? Is that where you met?"

Charlotte still said nothing.

"Bob drives across the country, hitting campus after campus. He has a whole network of dealers under him. I have to admit, I'm a little impressed with the guy. Very entrepreneurial. He's built an empire. But it's about to come crashing down."

"Who are you?" Charlotte whispered.

Regina shook her head. "I can't tell you that yet. But it doesn't matter. What matters is I've told you the truth."

After a long pause, Regina added: "Want the bottom line?"

"Yes," Charlotte heard herself say.

"One of two things is going to happen. Either Bob is going to continue doing what he's doing, or he's going to get caught. Which of those do you think it will be?"

Charlotte ran her fingers through her hair. Her hand trembled.

Regina noticed. "Listen," she added in a softer tone. "How long have you known this guy?"

"About a month," Charlotte lied. It was more like two weeks.

"Are you willing to spend years, maybe many years, in federal prison for somebody you just met?"

Charlotte felt some strength returning. She met Regina's gaze. "I just met you. Why should I trust you and not him?"

Regina surprised Charlotte with a smile. "The reference librarian said you had a list," Regina said.

"What?"

"Those books you wanted. Interlibrary loan. Right? The librarian told you that since you're not enrolled here, you can't use their interlibrary loan." Regina's eyes strayed to a neatly typed citation list on onion paper that lay among

Charlotte's many documents. Regina reached and picked up the list before Charlotte could stop her.

Regina whistled as she considered the titles. "1823. Man, you're not kidding around, are you?"

"May I have that back, please?" Charlotte asked in a freezing tone.

In response, Regina folded the thin paper, staring into Charlotte's eyes. "You're in luck. I'm enrolled at SDSU. It's night classes, but I have full library privileges. I'll get them for you."

Charlotte felt her face burning hot, but her tone descended into even icier depths: "If you don't give me my list back, it's theft."

Regina grinned. "It's on onion paper. I have a strong suspicion you have a copy. You seem thorough like that. Hey. Tell you what."

"What?" Charlotte asked despite herself.

"Why don't you do a little more nude sunbathing. Then we'll call it even." Regina rose from her seat. She looked Charlotte up and down, appraising the curves that the young scholar's caftan couldn't hide.

Then she walked away.

* * *

"Drugs?" Bob bellowed.

It had been two days since Charlotte's conversation with Regina. Charlotte had thought she would see Bob sooner. But Bob had not come home that night, nor the next night. He had originally warned her that he worked odd hours.

But she was starting to grow annoyed. And her annoyance had fueled her accusation, confronting Bob the moment he had walked in the door.

"Baby, hold on," he said. Closing his eyes, he hyperventilated.

Charlotte studied him. He had not shaved in a few days, nor changed his clothes.

"Okay," he finally continued. "Who exactly was this chick, where did you see her, what did she say, and what did you tell her?"

Charlotte omitted mentioning her first (naked) meeting with Regina on the deck—she felt weirdly self-conscious about it—but she told Bob everything about the library conversation.

He made an incredulous face. "And she's going to get you some books?"

Charlotte shrugged.

"Now what EXACTLY did she say about…me, and this marijuana thing?"

"I already told you. Do you want me to tell you again?"

Bob gave her a deadly look. "If I didn't, I wouldn't have asked."

She told him again.

Bob climbed the stairs to a floor that overlooked the Pacific Ocean through big wide windows. Heading straight to the wet bar, he uncorked a bottle of single malt and poured himself the better part of a tumbler.

"That's funny," Charlotte said.

He looked at her.

"I'm researching Scotch poets, and you drink scotch."

"Fuck you," he mumbled. He turned away and gulped the liquid.

Hurt, she waited before saying: "I was trying to lighten the mood."

"Great job."

She turned and walked into the kitchen.

After a half hour, Bob wandered in. He found Charlotte cutting vegetables. Her head was bowed and her shoulders were shaking.

He placed his hands gently upon her. "Baby."

"I didn't know what to do," she whispered. Sobs began pouring out of her, unstoppable.

"It's okay."

Turning her, he held her in his arms. She moved awkwardly, trying to keep the knife at arm's length.

"You know I don't do no drugs," Bob murmured. He kissed her hair.

"Ever?"

"No, sweet girl. All I do is sex."

Charlotte laughed, sniffling.

"Tomorrow I'm calling my lawyer. He's gonna get things straightened out." Bob kept talking, his anger rising, shouting about pigs and the Constitution. Minutes passed.

"How can I help?" Charlotte asked when he was finally done. She looked up with wet eyes.

Bob stared down at her with his wolfish grin. "Just what you've been doing, baby doll. Don't tell them nothing."

"Well, that's easy. You're not doing anything. So there's nothing to tell."

He seemed to consider this. Then he extracted himself from her embrace.

"What's wrong?" Charlotte asked.

"I better get some things out of the house."

"What things?"

"Aaah. Some stuff. No big deal."

As he turned to leave, Charlotte touched his arm. "Hey," she said. "If you haven't done anything…what's the matter?"

"Baby, it's the government. They set you up. If they're out to get you, they will do ANYTHING. They'll tell all kinds of lies, trying to get me…make me into something I'm not. Look, everybody breaks the law."

Bob spread his hands. "There's probably fifteen different laws we are breaking right now. There's probably a law about having an exhaust fan over the stove. But I don't have no fan over my stove. Right?"

Charlotte regarded the appliance uncertainly. "Right…"

"Well, there's one law I'm breaking. And there's probably a law about not having hubcaps on your car. And this, and that… And sooner or later, it all adds up, and there's one or two big ones that they can really hang you up on. So the less I have for them to get on me, the better, see?"

"Not really," Charlotte admitted.

"What don't you see?"

"I don't see how if you haven't done anything, why they would try to…'set you up.' Why would they care?"

"Baby, I'm a GAMBLER." He grinned his best slow, sexy smile. She couldn't help smiling back. "I'm doing my own thing, and even though technically it's not against the law, the law doesn't like it. Every single square, every single necktie-wearing robot who goes to church and pays taxes and obeys every rule in the book hates guys like me. I remind them of what they can't be. Guys like me, we are constantly under siege."

"I guess…"

"There you go. Hey. I love you."

Charlotte stood very still. He had never said the words before.

"I love you too," she said finally. It sounded like a question.

Bob kissed her and hurried out.

Two hours later he had crammed his car full of boxes and bulging plastic bags. He waved to Charlotte from the driveway before speeding off. She raised her hand to wave back, but he was gone.

* * *

Two weeks later, Charlotte walked out onto the house's back deck. Her hair had changed. She now had reddish-brown locks with red highlights.

Her bikini seemed oddly mismatched: orange top with black bottom. She carried a towel, a pitcher of iced tea, and a trashy novel.

As her bare feet touched the sun-warmed boards, she stopped short and smiled. "Hello."

Regina grinned back. She was leaning, as before, on the deck's rail with her feet on the sand. "I like your hair."

"Oh. Thanks." Charlotte touched it. "My new identity. I've gone underground."

"Seriously. It suits you."

"Seriously, I thank you. Even if my parents wouldn't. They don't know. They would wig out." Charlotte touched her hair once more, watching Regina.

Regina appraised Charlotte's bikini. "Black and orange. You a Cincinnati Bengals fan?"

Charlotte tugged at her top. "My chest is, uh…a little bigger than what's usual for my hips. So I had to buy two suits."

"It's expensive being you."

"I was wondering when I'd see you again."

Regina did a mock double-take. "So welcoming."

"Is that okay?"

"Welcoming is welcome."

"You're welcome."

The women smiled at each other.

Charlotte noticed Regina was also wearing a bikini. Navy blue with white polka dots. Regina's body looked hard and toned, with flat abs and sexy curves in her chest and butt.

Seeing Charlotte's stare, Regina touched her swimsuit. "Yeah. I'm actually off duty today."

"So this is a social call?"

"I guess you could say that."

"I'm flattered."

"You should be. Seriously, what's with the friendly attitude? I expected all kinds of aggro."

Charlotte frowned, making her nose wrinkle. It looked cute. "Aggro?"

"Aggression."

Charlotte shrugged. "I guess I'm just lonely."

"Oh, yeah?"

"Bob left two weeks ago. I haven't seen him or anybody else since."

"Let me guess: you finally told him about me."

"I didn't FINALLY tell him. I just…told him."

Regina nodded, pretending to be serious. "And now he's disappeared. Interesting."

"Where is he?"

"Let's talk about that later."

Charlotte stared at her feet. She looked vulnerable.

"Hey," Regina added. "You busy?"

"Not really." Charlotte held up her trashy novel. *His Every Desire*. It showed a bare-chested shirtless fellow crushing a bodice'd lady into his tanned flesh.

"Nice."

"I figured, since I couldn't get interlibrary loan,

you know, this would have to do."

"Is he Scottish?"

"I don't know. I haven't started it yet."

Regina nodded. "Don't pick up any bad habits."

Charlotte laughed. "Come on up."

"Love to, but can't."

"What? Why?"

"Legally, it's best if I don't actually step into the home. I'm not sure, but I have the feeling that stepping onto the deck counts."

"I see."

An awkward silence followed.

"But maybe you'd like a walk," Regina said.

Charlotte looked out at the ocean. It was a beautiful day. The beach was deserted.

"Let me get my sandals," she said.

Soon, Regina and Charlotte were strolling along a trace line of foam on cool wet sand.

"This is so nice," Charlotte said. She sighed with pleasure as a small wave lapped around her feet, then receded.

"Haven't you walked on the beach yet?"

"Not yet," Charlotte admitted. "Since that first day, when I met you, I guess I've been…a little spooked."

"There's no telling if Regina is lurking around every corner," Regina said in a scary voice.

"No, that's not it. I wasn't scared of you. I just…didn't know what else was out there."

They were quiet for a while.

"I like you," Regina said in an easy voice.

"I like you too," Charlotte said. "At least, as much as I can like someone who just shows up in my life and stalks me."

"You're welcome. Again." Regina's tone turned serious. "This is complicated."

"No kidding."

"Stop screwing around." As they walked, Regina reached without looking and held Charlotte's hand.

Charlotte inhaled sharply. She tried to gently pull her hand away, but Regina held it tight.

"The first minute I saw you, on that deck…" Regina's voice trailed off. She looked at the sea. Finally: "I said to myself, here I go. I'm throwing away my career. This time next year, I'll be working at Safeway, if I'm lucky."

"What are you talking about?" Charlotte stopped trying to pull her hand away.

"I was on surveillance duty that day. Somebody had the bright idea of watching both the front and the back of Bob's house. They only did it for a week. I pulled short straw on that one. Then budget realities came in, and they canceled the rear surveillance—"

Charlotte stopped walking. Regina was jerked to a halt, holding fast to her hand. "Just tell me," Charlotte said in a shaky voice. "Am I going to jail? Because of Bob?"

"That depends." Regina cocked her head, studying the beautiful face in front of her. "Did

Bob admit to you that he was engaged in illegal activity?"

"No."

"Have you engaged in any illegal activity since you have met him?"

"No."

"Did you even smoke a bong, or a roach, or anything whatsoever, in his house?"

"No! I'm not even sure what a roach is."

Regina laughed. "Okay. Then you're probably…"

"What?" Charlotte's hand tightened unconsciously around Regina's.

"Then you're probably fine."

"What the heck do you mean? 'Probably?' I haven't done anything!"

Regina shook her head. "There's plenty of people in prison who haven't done anything."

Charlotte wrenched her hand out of Regina's grasp.

"Listen to me," Regina continued. "I'm trying to help you. Remember?"

"Yeah. You liked me from the moment you saw me naked."

Regina looked away. "A hard point. But true." She gazed back at Charlotte.

"Where's Bob?" Charlotte asked.

Regina looked at her levelly. "If you really want to know, I'll tell you. But ask yourself if you really want to know. If you're questioned, it will be a lot easier for you if you just stick to the truth and say what you knew when you knew it. Trust me, cops can smell liars from a mile away."

"I don't understand any of this."

"Do you want me to tell you where Bob is?"

Charlotte looked down at the sand. Remains of the waves washed over her feet. She sighed. The joy had gone. "I guess not."

"Can you leave Bob's house? Today?"

Charlotte looked up. "And go where?"

"Anywhere."

"I don't have a car. I don't have money for a hotel. Much less a plane ticket. Where am I supposed to go?"

Regina shrugged. "I can't exactly invite you to my place. Much as I would like to."

"Don't worry. Never gonna happen."

"Don't be so proud."

"Excuse me?"

Regina reached and touched Charlotte's face with a tender hand. Charlotte didn't move. "You're so beautiful," Regina whispered. "Beautiful things grow in protected spaces. I bet where you grew up, you didn't need protection."

"Appleton, Wisconsin can be pretty rough," Charlotte said, trying to keep her voice light. Regina's touch made her skin tingle all over.

Regina did not smile. "I really feel like kissing you right now."

"What would Bob say?"

This time, Regina did smile. She took Charlotte's hand once more and tugged. Charlotte walked with her, unresisting.

After a while, they came upon a parking lot higher up on the shore. "This is where I'm parked," Regina said.

Charlotte looked surprised. "Oh."

"Like I told you: the front of your house may or may not be watched. And if I'm off duty, I can't exactly approach from the front. Know what I mean?"

"Not exactly."

"God, when are you going to go back to Wisconsin or wherever you're from?"

Charlotte seemed hurt. "Don't be mean."

"I was kidding!"

The blonde giggled and punched Regina's shoulder with her free hand. "Gotcha."

"Bitch."

"That's what they call me."

"You're a terrible liar. Why don't you let me give you a ride back to your house?"

Regina's beat-up Ford smelled like French fries. "How do you stay in such good shape eating junk food?" Charlotte asked as she slid a lap seatbelt over her bikini.

"On my salary, I ain't exactly doing Cordon Bleu. Plus, I'm a runner."

Charlotte spied an envelope among the clutter on the passenger floorboard: *Summons*. On the return address: *San Diego County Sheriff's Department*.

Regina noticed Charlotte reading.

Charlotte looked at her.

"Cat's out of the bag now, huh?" Regina said.

Charlotte nodded slowly. "I guessed it was either that, DEA, or FBI."

"I interviewed with the Feds before I took this job. But Feds apparently don't like to see a woman carrying a gun. Maybe that will change. But the Sheriff's Department is cool."

Charlotte looked at her with real interest. "Do you like it?"

Regina grinned. "It's pretty great."

After driving some ways, Regina pulled over under the shade of a short small tree.

"Why are we stopping here?" Charlotte asked.

"This taxi only goes so far. Sorry. Bob's house is being watched. I don't want to have to explain to my supervisors tomorrow why I was out on a date with the moll of the guy we're surveilling."

"I'm not a moll…"

Regina's lips were on hers. Charlotte's eyes opened wide, then fluttered shut. With a sure hand, Regina unlatched both their seatbelts. Charlotte felt Regina's arms slide around her and pull her close.

After a moment, the resistance went out of Charlotte's body, like it had on the beach after she had tried to pull away from Regina's hand-holding. She accepted the kiss passively.

Regina pulled away ever so slightly and gave Charlotte's sea-spray-salt lips a fast little lick.

Surprised, Charlotte opened her mouth

slightly. Regina crushed her own mouth upon it and forced her tongue inside.

Charlotte felt a hand sliding up from her knee.

"No," she tried to say. But the word did not come out. And, anyway, Regina had clamped her mouth firmly over hers.

Charlotte held Regina's wrist, straining to keep the brunette's hand at bay. But Regina maintained a constant pressure of her own, touching Charlotte's pale thighs and sliding her fingertips in and out of the squeezed place between her passenger's knees.

Regina kept kissing Charlotte. A car passed. Neither woman opened her eyes to look.

Finally, Charlotte's resisting arm sagged. Regina slid her hand up Charlotte's legs and began rubbing gentle circles on the triangle of bikini fabric above Charlotte's mons.

"Oh," Charlotte gasped.

"God," Regina whispered. "You are gonna get me fired for sure." With a quick movement she bent her head into her passenger's lap, pulled down Charlotte's bikini bottom a little with a finger and shoved her tongue deep into her thatch of blonde pubic hair.

Charlotte's back arched against her seat. Her head hit the car's ceiling as she jumped, yelling.

Regina pulled back, concerned. "Are you okay?"

Charlotte rubbed her head. "Define 'okay,'" she moaned.

Regina grinned. "Guess that's a sign. No more for you."

Charlotte blinked. "Ever?"

"Today, silly. One of the stakeout guys is bound to drive by here sooner or later, if that wasn't them who passed already. But I really shouldn't be fooling around with you anyway." She tapped the passenger door. "I'm afraid I'm going to have to ask you to leave."

Charlotte opened the door and stepped out, her brain spinning.

As she walked away, Regina stuck her head out the driver's window. "Hey."

Charlotte hurried back. Bending down for a kiss, she instead received a heavy grocery bag through the window.

"I almost forgot," Regina said. "Your books."

"Oh. Thanks."

"You don't look too excited."

"I was kind of enjoying having an excuse to not write my dissertation."

"I can keep them for you if you want."

"No, I'll take them. Thank you. Really."

"You're welcome." As Charlotte hefted the grocery bag of books, she felt something on her hip. She looked. Regina was tracing her finger down, a slow, sensuous journey.

Charlotte looked up again. "I guess it goes without saying, but: I've never done anything like this with a girl before."

"In that case, you're a natural. Hey. Do me a

favor. Put those books in your suitcase, and attach a tag with your name on the suitcase, all right?"

"Why?"

"Just trust me."

Charlotte gazed at her. "I do trust you."

Regina grinned. Then she drove away.

Charlotte carried the books five blocks back to Bob's house.

*   *   *

Very early the next morning, Charlotte's eyes snapped open. She turned in her bed. Someone was pounding at the front door.

She looked out the window. The sun had not yet appeared.

Rising out of bed, she switched on the overhead light. The pounding on the door grew louder. "All right, I'm coming," she shouted down the stairs. She dressed a t-shirt, jeans and sandals before hurrying down the stairs.

"Who is it?" she asked at the door.

A man's voice on the threshold responded: "FBI."

Shaking, Charlotte opened the door.

Thirty minutes later, she was sitting on a bench attached to a wall in a small room within a nondescript building. She rubbed her wrists. Her handcuffs had just been removed.

Two middle-aged white men in suits entered, carrying thick folders. They looked as clean-cut as preachers. The men closed the door and walked to the other side of a table sitting in the middle of the room. They did not look at Charlotte.

"Hello?" Charlotte asked. She tried to keep her voice from catching. She had cried more in the last half-hour than she had ever cried in her life.

The men sat down, removed some documents from their folders, and whispered between themselves. Then they finally acknowledged the frightened woman sitting in the room. "Would you care to sit with us?" one said, indicating the single chair on the other side of the table.

In short order, the men introduced themselves. They belonged to a special FBI investigative task force. And they wanted to know all about Bob Custis.

Charlotte took a deep breath. *They can smell liars,* she thought. *That's what Regina told you.*

Charlotte decided to tell them everything she knew, with the exception of meeting Regina.

Two hours later, the FBI agents kept returning to the topic of Charlotte's last discussion with Bob.

"So you suspected that he was a drug smuggler?"

"Yes."

"Why did you think that?"

Charlotte paused. She didn't want to bring Regina into it. An idea came to her. She lifted her head and looked at them proudly. "A woman has intuition."

The men glanced at each other.

"You can ask your wives," Charlotte added.

"And he denied being a drug smuggler?" one of the agents asked, irritated.

"Yes. Vehemently."

The men began questioning her about things, people, and places that Charlotte had never heard of. Her bafflement seemed to amuse them.

"So you never met, or heard anyone speak of, Francisco 'Greasy Gun' Guzman?"

Charlotte's jaw dropped. "'Greasy Gun' GUZMAN?"

"Okay, I didn't think so." The agent made a note.

Charlotte took a deep breath and closed her eyes. "Listen. I have tried to help you as much as I can. Am I under arrest?"

"You better believe you're under arrest."

Charlotte's eyes bugged. "For WHAT?"

The agents looked at each other. "How about conspiracy?" one said.

"For openers." The other man nodded.

"But that's...that's ridiculous," Charlotte stuttered. "I didn't do anything. I didn't know anything."

"If you will just answer our questions, we will try to help you as much as we can."

Charlotte folded her arms. "I have already told you everything. Is your game trying to get me to repeat things over and over, so you can catch me in a lie?"

The agents glanced at each other again, raising their eyebrows.

"I am not lying to you. And if you are placing me under arrest, after I've tried to help you as much as I can, then you don't trust me. So I see no reason to trust you. I'm not going to speak to you any more. I want an attorney."

The agents shrugged. Their body language indicated that they could care less. Rising, they slipped their notes and documents back into their folders before leaving without a word.

* * *

Much later that evening, Regina walked down the long hall of the confinement wing in the San Diego County Jail. Female prisoners shouted, sang, and screamed from within the cells she passed.

Arriving at the main holding area, Regina scanned the large room behind steel bars. She spotted Charlotte. The Wisconsin girl was still in the clothes she had thrown on that morning. She stood with her back against the wall, surrounded by tough-looking women.

Regina withdrew her keys from her pocket and banged on the bars. "Hey!"

The women inside the cell turned and looked.

"You." Regina pointed at Charlotte. "Beauty Queen. Over here, now. The rest of you, stay the fuck away."

Charlotte hurried over to the bars. The other

prisoners watched her leave, muttering and winking among themselves.

"Oh my God," Charlotte whispered. She clutched the bars, pushing her face as far toward Regina as possible. "I've been wondering where you were."

"Sorry," Regina whispered back. She glanced around. "I've been doing my best. Hey. What did you tell the Feds?"

"You mean the FBI?"

"Is that who questioned you?"

"Yeah."

"Shit." Regina sighed. "I was hoping it would be DEA. The FBI guys are worse. Okay, so what did you tell them?"

"The truth," Charlotte whispered. "Except about meeting you, of course. What's going on? Did they catch Bob?"

"Bob's disappeared. Gone. He crossed to Mexico two weeks ago, and they lost his trail. They're scared they're going to lose him forever. That's why they're leaning so hard on you. They think you may know where he is."

"WHAT?"

"Calm down."

Charlotte started to cry.

"Stop it. Stop it!" Regina hissed. "The last thing you want the girls in here thinking is that you're weak."

"I AM weak," Charlotte said, sniffling. She wiped her nose.

"Then pretend. Hey. Want some good news?"

"You mean there is some?"

"I sort of greased the wheels and got them to set bail for you. Usually it takes longer."

"Bail? How much?"

Regina looked around again, making sure there were no eavesdroppers. Then she sighed. "It's a big number. A lot of cash. But it's doable. You can walk out of here tonight."

Charlotte gripped the bars so tightly her fingers turned white. "Really?"

"Yeah." Regina withdrew a small pad and a pen from a pocket. "Give me the number of someone who can pay a bail bondsman."

Charlotte looked panicked. "I don't… I don't know anyone who has any money."

"This is serious."

"Gee, thanks. I didn't realize." Charlotte somehow gripped the bars even harder. "I'M serious. My parents live on a tiny farm that their bank owns. My dad's a great farmer but a terrible businessman. He's in debt. Nobody in my family owns anything…my friends are all artists or scholars."

"Isn't there somebody? Anybody?"

Charlotte thought hard. "Maybe my dissertation advisor. Dr. Wainwright. I think he has made some money from his books…but I don't know. I'd hate to bother him."

"Would you prefer to stay here for a while?"

"No." Charlotte shivered.

"Okay. He's in Madison, right? Where you go to school?"

Charlotte nodded.

"What's his first and middle name?"

"Jeffrey K. Wainwright. I don't know what his middle initial stands for."

"I'll be right back." Then Regina shouted so the other prisoners could hear: "I know you killed those women! You're the most sick, psychotic bitch I've ever known!"

Regina left.

An hour later, she returned. Charlotte was waiting by the bars this time.

Regina glared at some street women in the cell who had been hovering around Charlotte. The women sauntered away.

"They keep calling me 'White Girl,'" Charlotte whispered. "I think I'm in danger!"

"You know, you would make me laugh, under other circumstances. So I called that guy, Dr. Wainwright. I got his home number in Madison."

Charlotte rose on her tip-toes. "And?"

"Lots of sympathy. No money."

"Oh, God."

"I pushed as hard as I could. He says he doesn't have it."

Charlotte started to cry again.

"BUT."

Charlotte blinked her wet eyes. "But?"

"You're still getting bailed out of here in ten minutes."

"I…am?"

"Seems this is your lucky night."

"I can't do irony right now. How? What happened?"

"I'll tell you soon. Listen. On the form you sign when you leave, you have to put down an address. Just write 'Transient.' It means you're homeless."

"Okay…"

"Obviously you can't go back to Bob's house. And under the terms of your bail, you cannot leave San Diego county, much less the state. So going home to Wisconsin isn't exactly an option for you."

"Okay." Charlotte seemed desperate to agree to whatever Regina wanted.

"When you walk out of here, go five blocks north, straight up the avenue. You'll see a Der Weinerschnitzel. I'll be in the parking lot."

An hour later, Charlotte wandered into a dark area behind a high-roofed stand that sold hot dogs during open hours. The place was closed.

"Over here."

Charlotte approached, letting her eyes adjust to the gloom. Regina was leaning against her beat-up Ford.

"Thank you so much," Charlotte began.

"Forget it."

"Who put up the bail?"

"A guy called Jimmy. He owns a bail bond business across the street from the jail. You may have noticed it when you walked out. I send a lot of business his way. He likes me. Even so, I had to sign over my house, my car, my wages, and damn near the shirt off my back for him to take you on, with that high dollar bail the Feds set. I guaranteed Jimmy you wouldn't skip."

"Thank you so much," Charlotte repeated.

"You're welcome."

"So you lost your house?"

"Well, no. I just signed a promise to give it to Jimmy if anything goes wrong with your bond. But I'm guessing you won't run away and forfeit the bond. Right?"

Charlotte began crying again.

Regina tried to roll her eyes, but she looked concerned. "What's wrong? You're out."

"I feel so GODDAMNED STUPID." Charlotte shook her head, wiping her face on her sleeve. "Why did I ever hook up with that guy? Why didn't I take your advice and get out of there when I could?"

"What's done is done. Let's focus on the future."

"Right." Charlotte sniffed, and stood straighter.

"First: do you have any money or ID?"

"No. This morning they handcuffed me and threw me into a car in like sixty seconds flat. My purse is back at the house."

"No it's not."

"What do you mean?"

Regina made a face. "The house and everything in it was taken into custody. Your purse is probably in an evidence warehouse somewhere."

Charlotte looked down. "I never thought I could cry so much that I couldn't cry any more."

"Where will you sleep tonight?"

Charlotte sighed. "I guess I'll find a shelter."

"The ones I know close their doors at eight."

"What time is it?"

"Eleven."

Charlotte buried her face in her hands.

Regina regarded her for a long time. "You can stay with me," she said finally. "On two conditions."

Charlotte looked up, stunned. "You would do that? Really?"

"First condition: you and me don't fool around. No kissing, nothing. I'm already in deep enough as it is. If the Feds find out I'm helping you, it will not be good for me. At all. So we need to keep everything professional. Might be too late for that, but anyway. You might not believe it, but I have some professional ethics issues in this, personally, as well."

Charlotte nodded. "I agree. What's the other thing?"

"Tomorrow, you get a job."

"What?"

Regina ticked off her fingers as if making a shopping list. "You need a lawyer. Specifically,

Marty Finkelstein. I have had cases where I was certain the perp was going down for life and Marty bargained it down to misdemeanor. The lawyer is good. But because he is, he's expensive. I called him at home while you were in lockup. But his retainer went up this year, 1972. Five thousand dollars."

"FIVE THOUSAND?" Charlotte took a step back. "I could buy a house in Appleton for that much!"

"Yeah. Only you wouldn't get to live there. Because you would be doing twenty to life in the federal pen."

A street-looking man approached them in the darkness. "Hey, ladies. How you doing tonight?"

Regina opened her jacket, showing her badge and her gun. "Fuck off."

"Yes, MA'AM," the man said. He disappeared.

"Are you listening to me?" Regina asked Charlotte.

"Uh. Yeah. Yeah," she responded.

"The lawyer needs a retainer. But you don't have any money. I sure as hell don't have any after paying Jimmy. So you need a loan. But banks are not in the habit of loaning money to homeless, unemployed women. So here's what you do. Remember the University of San Diego?"

Charlotte recalled the beautiful campus with its Spanish-style Mission architecture. "Of course."

"I'll give you the last cash out of my wallet. You buy some nice clothes tomorrow. You take the bus. Go to the human resources department at USD. Look at the job listings, full-time vacant positions. Find something you think you can get, fast. Secretary, office manager, something."

Regina looked around, checking for observers. "Once you've found the job listings, find somewhere on campus where you can type up a quick resume. A student lounge with a typewriter, something. List your contacts at the University of Wisconsin as references. USD will like that, universities always like each other. Then go back to human resources and put in your application. Apply for as many jobs as you can. Once you're employed, you will go to the university credit union and take out a personal loan for whatever you can get. You'll also apply for as many credit cards as possible, so you can take out cash advances. You scrape five thousand together. Then you take the money to Marty."

Charlotte groaned. She was feeling very tired. This had been the longest, scariest, craziest day of her life. "I don't see why need a lawyer. I didn't DO anything. I'm innocent."

"Why didn't you tell the FBI that?"

"I did!"

"Exactly."

Regina let that sink in.

"The Feds don't care if you're innocent or guilty," Regina finally continued. "Okay? You got that? You keep telling me what you've done or not done. I am telling you, IT DOES NOT

MATTER. What matters is that Bob has vanished. And it's making the Feds look stupid."

Regina stretched. "That's why they knocked on your door this morning. They're scared they've lost him forever. And if they just write this off, with no convictions, somebody up the food chain is going to be looking at the ledger and saying that the guys on this case are all a bunch of fuck-ups. So the guys want a conviction. It can be you, or somebody else. But right now it looks like there isn't somebody else."

"That's horrible," Charlotte stuttered. "What kind of justice is this?"

"Welcome to the real world." She yawned. "I'm tired. I'm going home. Are you coming?"

Charlotte thought about it. "So, no fooling around with you, and I have to go to USD and apply for a job tomorrow?"

"Unless you have a better idea for somewhere you can work. Der Wienerschnitzel might be hiring." Regina thumbed at the hot dog stand. "But I'm not sure they have a credit union."

Sighing, Charlotte asked: "Can we at least stop somewhere on the way and you buy me a toothbrush?"

Regina grinned. "Let's go."

After picking up the toothbrush, they drove to Escondido. Regina's home was a classic 1920s Sears Roebuck prefab house, of a type that dotted many San Diego neighborhoods.

Charlotte was ravenous. She had not eaten all

day. Regina cooked a quick pot of spaghetti. After dinner, the host left the table before returning with folded pajamas.

"My sister left them behind," Regina said. "They may fit you."

Charlotte shook them out. Teddy-bear print. She looked up with a sunny smile. "Thank you."

"You know," Regina said, "you don't look like someone who's been through what you've been through today."

"I recover quickly." Charlotte shrugged. "It's the Norwegian in me. We are a stoic people."

"Yeah? I guess Italians like me could learn something from you. We just get pissed off and scream. Ready for bed?"

In the living room, Charlotte stretched out on the couch. Regina fetched her a pillow and blanket. "Sorry," Regina said. "I don't get many visitors."

"That's fine." Charlotte gazed at service awards and plaques on the wall. Regina was a highly decorated officer.

"Feel free to leave the TV on if you can't sleep. You won't bother me."

"Thanks."

"This is the part where we say good night."

Charlotte smiled. "I guessed."

"And I really want to kiss you."

"Sounds dangerous. I remember what happened the last time you said that."

"Yeah. Which is why I'm turning around and

going to bed."

"Better safe than sorry."

"I'm leaving now."

"Lingering."

"Bitch."

"That's what they call me."

Regina grinned despite herself. She turned, walked her bedroom, and closed the door.

Hours later, Regina emerged again. She wore a long shirt that reached to her knees.

Charlotte looked up. She was in the teddy-bear PJs, sitting on the floor with her back to the couch. The TV was on.

The blonde smiled. "Hey."

"Hey."

"Did the television wake you?"

Regina shook her head. "Couldn't sleep."

"Me neither."

"Can I join you?"

"Please."

Regina approached the couch. She lifted her leg and turned as if mounting a horse. Lowering, she sat on the cushions with Charlotte's shoulders between her knees. "What are you watching?"

"Benny Hill. It's the only thing on."

"Want some breakfast? It'll be light soon."

"No, thanks. I'm enjoying this show. I've never seen Benny Hill before."

Regina looked. A middle-aged man on the black-and-white TV glanced out from behind some bushes. He leered up at an oblivious girl on a balcony. She smiled, discarded her robe, and stepped inside. For a split second, there was a flash of breast.

"I can't believe this," Charlotte said. "Nudity on television! Why don't the censors catch it?"

"Maybe it's the hour. No kids are up this late. Or this early, whichever." Rachel placed her hands upon Charlotte's shoulders.

"It's still pretty crazy. In Wisconsin, if you saw stuff like this on TV, people would be burning down the State House."

"Remind me to visit Wisconsin. It sounds like fun." Regina began a gentle massage.

"Don't talk that way about my state…oh, my gosh. Also, don't stop."

"Okay."

"Can you do that a little harder?" Charlotte groaned.

"Sure. Can you scoot forward a bit?"

Charlotte obeyed. Regina slid down to sit on the floor where Charlotte had been, splaying her legs wider to fit her facing-away guest between them.

"How much do you charge?" Charlotte asked. She sighed as Regina massaged her back. "Whatever it is, I can afford it."

"My rates are very reasonable."

Charlotte said nothing. She closed her eyes and bowed her head.

After a few minutes, Regina's hands slid under Charlotte's arms. Regina cupped her breasts gently.

"Oh, my," Charlotte murmured.

"Too forward?"

"Extremely."

"You'll have to call the police."

"I haven't had good luck with them lately."

Regina began unbuttoning Charlotte's pajama top: a slow, deliberate undressing.

"I guess," Charlotte said in a shaky voice, "that that first condition of me staying here is sort of…"

"Yeah."

"Kiss me."

Charlotte turned her chin, closing her eyes. Regina kissed her as lightly as anyone had ever been kissed. Her hands pulled the pajama top open. Regina placed her palms over Charlotte's hard nipples.

"Oh," Charlotte gasped. Regina crushed her lips into her guest's, silencing her.

Then a wind-up alarm clock rang from inside Regina's bedroom.

"I don't BELIEVE this," Regina said.

Charlotte opened her eyes. "What?"

"I set my alarm for the very last minute. The very. I have to go to work."

"You're kidding…right?"

"Two things I don't joke about: football, and work." The alarm clock's *brrriiing* died a slow death as its wind-up spring slackened.

Regina stood up. Charlotte began to button

her top. Her head was bowed.

"Better this way, anyway." Regina said. "We shouldn't start off like this."

Charlotte looked up, then down again. "You make the rules."

*   *   *

That night when Regina arrived home, she heard the television playing. Regina pulled off her jacket and set it on a peg next to the door. Then she walked into the living room.

Charlotte was in her pajamas on the couch. She looked up from watching television.

"Hey," Charlotte said.

"Hey."

A long, awkward pause followed.

Regina folded her arms. "So. How was your day?"

"Fine. I'm using your washing machine. I hope you don't mind. I wanted to wash my clothes. I had to do a separate load for the blouse. It's cold-water-wash only."

"Blouse?"

"My business shirt." Charlotte turned back to the television. "The suit itself is dry clean."

Regina seemed to relax. "Then…"

"No, I have not been here all day watching TV."

"I didn't say that."

"Your eyes spoke volumes."

Regina looked puzzled. "Are you mad at me?"

Charlotte groaned. She rubbed her face. "I have no right to be. You are letting me stay here. You are being incredibly…giving. I really appreciate everything."

"But you're angry, anyway."

Charlotte looked up at her again. "You have to admit: this morning was a little rough."

"I'm SORRY."

"Damn right." Charlotte turned back to the television.

Regina raised her hands high, as if the victim of a stick-up. "What the hell is wrong with you?"

"What the hell is wrong with YOU? You tell me no fooling around. Then you fool around. Then you tell me no. Again. Fucking make up your mind."

"Whoa." Regina pretended to be hit by a bullet, staggering back with her hand to her chest. "I thought 'heck' was bad language, for you."

"It seems I've been corrupted." Charlotte turned back to the television.

"Can I sit with you?"

The blonde shifted on the couch, making room. Regina joined her.

"So how did it go today?" the host asked. Regina tried not to look at Charlotte's pajama top. Through a cavity between two buttons, a bit of milky breast was visible.

"Fine. I took the money you left on the kitchen table. I bought a nice suit. UCD had a bunch of open positions. I applied for a lot, like you said."

"That's great."

"Yeah. And they told me, off the record, that I'd probably get a call in the next few days."

"That's super great."

"I put your address and phone number on the applications, of course."

"Of course. Hey, I can take you to DMV this weekend. You can get a driver's license, so that you'll be ready with ID when they hire you."

"Cool. Thanks."

Silence.

"Okay," Regina sighed. "Let's talk."

Charlotte rose, turned off the television, and returned to the couch. The women sat facing each other.

Regina began. "I'm more attracted to you...then I ever thought I could be, to anyone. The second I saw you, lying naked on that deck? Before I knew what was happening, I was walking over the sand...straight to you. Blew the surveillance. Blew my cover. Didn't even think."

Regina looked down at her feet. Her toughness had been stripped away. She looked scared and vulnerable. "I'm really...I'm the kind of person who doesn't like to get hurt. And, honestly, I have already fallen for you. And if you...leave me, it will hurt."

Charlotte studied her. "Why didn't you just say that in the first place?"

"You mean, in the Der Weinerschnitzel

parking lot?"

"Yeah. In the Der Weinerschnitzel parking lot," Charlotte said. She did not smile.

Regina looked away. "I don't have a good answer for you. I… Why don't you say something now."

Charlotte paused before speaking. "I don't know if I'm going to leave you. I don't know if I'm going to stay."

Regina nodded.

"I'm sorry," Charlotte continued. "You told me once: be honest. Because people like you can smell dishonesty. Right?"

Regina still said nothing.

"This is all… I mean, consider it from my perspective. I have never even kissed a girl before. I have never wanted to before. But kissing you feels good. Wait, let me finish. This thing—I mean, I am looking at prison. Prison! And I just feel desperate and needy, and…I don't know if that is coloring how I feel about you, or not."

"I've wondered about that, too," Regina said quietly.

"But this business about 'don't fool around,' and then you're kissing me, and then you're saying it's wrong: that has got to stop."

Regina started to cry.

"It's not fair," Charlotte said firmly. "Either it's one way or the other. Otherwise, it's not eight o'clock yet. I will find a shelter. I already looked a few up."

"Then why aren't you gone?" Regina asked, wiping her eyes.

"Just tell me. What you want?"

"I'm thinking," Regina said.

Charlotte waited.

"Okay," Regina said finally. "Here it is. I know the best thing, for me anyway, is for us to leave each other alone. But just being around you—I can't. It's too strong." She looked down and reached for Charlotte's hand. "If you stay here, it's going to happen, sooner or later. Probably sooner."

"Awfully presumptuous, aren't you? What about what I want?"

Regina opened her mouth to apologize.

"I'm kidding," Charlotte said. "I don't do anything I don't want to do."

"Yeah. So, that's my spiel." Regina looked away, unable to meet Charlotte's gaze. "What do you think?"

"I think...I'm ready to share your bed. But I'm not ready to promise I'm never going to leave. I can't. I just can't."

Regina nodded. "I think that's fair. I'm sure it's fair. Who knows, I might even leave you."

"Bitch."

Regina tried to smile. "That's what they call me."

Charlotte looked thoughtful. "Can we just let this...develop? Organically? I don't really know what this is yet. But I'm attracted to you."

Regina's face seemed to light up from within. "You mean it?"

"Yeah."

"Oh, wow. That is…that is the best news I've ever heard in my life."

Charlotte smiled. "Who would've known you were so gushy?"

Regina stood up. "Come with me."

Charlotte rose also. Regina led her by the hand to the bedroom.

However, at the bedroom threshold, Regina stopped.

"What's wrong?" Charlotte asked.

Regina turned to her so slowly it seemed like she was hardly turning it all. "I feel weak."

"Don't."

"I do. I feel weak because it's true. Right now I AM weak."

Charlotte squeezed her hand. "It's okay."

"No, it's not." Regina shook her head. "Being strong is who I am—it's my identity. My pride. And you know what? I cried just now. I haven't cried since eighth grade."

Charlotte began to speak.

"Listen," Regina said, cutting her off. "I'm not playing with you. I'm saying I'm making a decision. You don't want any more mixed signals from me—I get it." Regina inhaled and stood straighter. "So we stick to the original plan. No fooling around."

Charlotte's jaw dropped. "Ever?"

Regina laughed. "You look so disappointed."

"Don't joke."

"I want you, more than you know. But not like this. It's not good for me, and it's not good for you. Look, I'm not asking for a declaration of love. But if all this gets resolved, with the Feds, you'll either go home or you will stick around—for a little while, at least."

Charlotte looked at the floor. Regina squeezed her hand.

The host continued: "If you go home, we part as friends. I hope. I may still have a broken heart, but, you know, it'll be easier for me to bear. And if you don't go home…"

"Yes?"

"Maybe we can share a bed then."

Charlotte cocked her head. "Maybe?"

"Yeah, well. One hundred percent certain."

"That's better."

"Indeed."

Charlotte exhaled loudly. "Okay. Then what about tonight?"

"I have some chicken in the fridge."

"Talk about an anticlimax. My heart just now was racing so fast I thought I would pass out."

"Glad I wasn't the only one. You hungry?"

Charlotte grinned. "For food?"

They laughed. Then they turned around and headed for the kitchen. "So what happened that made you cry in eighth grade?" Charlotte asked.

"My science project broke. It was the night

before the fair."

"Tough break."

"Tell me about it. Especially when I had been gluing toothpicks for weeks, making a model of water molecules."

"Then what happened?"

"Billy Fitzpatrick won. Exactly what I didn't want to happen. I've never gotten over it."

"I've noticed you can be a little intense sometimes."

"Yeah? Just wait till the NFL playoffs."

They passed into the kitchen.

* * *

Months went by. Regina kept her word.

However, it had not been easy. After a couple of weeks of enduring Regina's inattention, Charlotte had walked into the living room one weekend wearing a towel that barely hid anything.

Regina had looked up from her book. She had glared. "What the hell are you doing?"

Charlotte's eyebrows had lifted innocently. "I thought this was my room."

"What the hell are you doing?" Regina had repeated.

Charlotte had shrugged. "I just needed my clothes…"

"You're not allowed to torture me. I'm keeping my promise. I think I'm doing pretty well."

"Mmm-hmm!" Charlotte had pretended to

agree vigorously.

"Flouncing around like that may be funny to you, but it's killing me."

"I don't know what you're talking about."

Regina had jumped up from the couch and yanked off Charlotte's towel. Charlotte had gasped, bent over, and had tried to cover her jiggling nakedness with her arms. "What the hell!"

"Get out of here!"

Giggling, Charlotte had run away back to the bedroom. Regina had pursued her, cracking her heart-shaped ass with the towel. Charlotte had shrieked, bolted inside the bathroom, and locked the door. When she had finally emerged, she found a note from Regina saying that Regina had gone to a friend's house to take a cold shower.

It had only taken a few days for Charlotte to land a job at USD. The music department hired her as an office and events coordinator. Charlotte liked the work, and the people.

In short order, she had pulled together enough money to pay Marty Finkelstein his retainer. Charlotte had nicknamed him "The Godfather," both for his remarkable resemblance to the title character in that new movie, and for the deference with which his staff treated him. Finklestein had immediately begun demanding of the US Attorney that they set a trial date. The US Attorney had kept stalling.

And now, months after Charlotte's arrest, Regina was taking her—them—on a vacation.

Charlotte let her foot dangle out the passenger window of Regina's Ford. The wind blew in her hair—she had gone back to her natural blonde.

"So what is this place?" Charlotte asked. She had packed a bag. Her personal possessions were slowly growing. They included a pretty high-collar sundress that she had worn on this trip.

"You'll see," Regina said.

Charlotte gave her sidelong look. "Is there one bed?"

"You'll see."

Charlotte turned her head, looked out the window and smiled.

The bed and breakfast in Santa Cruz sat on a lonely hilltop overlooking the ocean.

"You are the only guests this weekend," said the owner, an ancient woman. Her guests signed the register. It was mid-afternoon.

Charlotte looked around as they entered the room. A beautiful four-poster bed sported a gigantic comforter and big puffy pillows. A heavy antique mirror in a wood frame hung on the wall across the room in front of the bed. Under the ocean-facing window was a cot.

Regina pointed at the cot. "I'll sleep there."

Charlotte made a face. "It doesn't seem fair. You're paying for this, after all."

"Yeah, well."

The phone rang.

Regina and Charlotte looked at each other.

"Did you tell anyone we were coming here?"

Charlotte asked.

"I told the department. But that's procedure. They've never called me before on my time off."

"Oh, no."

"It's okay," Regina said as she moved toward the lime-green rotary telephone. "It's probably just the lady downstairs, telling us where the extra blankets are." Regina picked up the receiver. "Hello?"

After a moment, she locked eyes with Charlotte. "Hello, Marty."

Charlotte mouthed the words: *my lawyer?*

Regina nodded back. "Not disturbing us at all, no. Is everything all right?" A few seconds passed. Then Regina held out the receiver to Charlotte. "He wants to talk to you."

"What?"

"He tried you at work. They told him you'd gone on vacation. Then he tried calling ME at work. The department told him the same thing. So he sweet-talked them into giving the number where I could be reached."

Charlotte gaped. "Isn't that against the law?"

"Ask him. He's the lawyer. C'mon, my arm is getting tired."

Charlotte walked over and took the phone. "Hello?"

Regina left the room, giving Charlotte some privacy.

Returning later, Regina said as she opened the door: "I saw the greatest restaurant next door…"

Charlotte surprised her with a run-up-hug.

"Whoa!" Regina said.

"I'm free!"

"What?"

Charlotte explained. Marty had news. Bob had been captured somewhere in Latin America, and was being extradited to San Diego. He was denying everything.

Unfortunately for law enforcement, Bob had been very thorough about covering his tracks.

However…the Feds thought that if they could tie Bob to the marijuana-transporting Winnebago, which was now in their custody, they might have a case. They had not found any of Bob's fingerprints on the vehicle—it had been cleaned very well. That was where Charlotte came in.

"Marty says that if I testify that that Winnebago belongs to Bob, the government will drop all the charges against me," Charlotte said in a rush.

"Can you?"

"I'd know that camper anywhere. It has a little Keep On Truckin' sticker on the rear bumper, and a dent on the right side of the door where somebody probably kicked it. Bob never let me inside, but I know his Winnebago."

"Why do the Feds care so much about it?"

Charlotte jumped up and down in her excitement. "They have plenty of people who remember the Winnebago, and somebody selling really big amounts of weed out of it. But nobody can testify specifically that it was Bob. He changed his appearance a lot, it seems."

Regina grinned. "Also, the witnesses might have been high at the time."

"Good point."

"So, that's it?"

"Yeah. I thought you would be happy for me."

"I am. I am!" Regina wrapped her arms around Charlotte and held her tight.

Charlotte looked uncertain. "Hey…are you crying?"

"Happy."

Extracting herself, Charlotte studied the other woman. "You sure?"

"Yeah." Regina wiped her face.

"Waaaaiiiit a minute." Charlotte's eyes narrowed. "Marty said they arrested Bob two days ago."

"Okay. So?"

"Did you know that?"

Regina shrugged and looked away.

Charlotte took a step back. "Did you know he wasn't talking? Did you know—"

"Okay. Yes. Yes!" Regina rolled her eyes. "I heard on the inside that the Feds were going to offer you the deal. Okay? I thought… I thought it would be nice to be up here when you heard the news." Regina looked away again. "I wanted it to be a surprise."

Charlotte's eyes softened. "Then why are you upset?"

"It's just…" Regina turned and sat on the bed. "I'm happy for you. So, so happy. You have no idea. But…"

Nodding slowly, Charlotte sat next to Regina. "But now that this has happened, there's nothing to stop me from going home to Wisconsin."

"You should do whatever you want to do." Regina tried to smile.

After a long pause, Charlotte said: "I have an idea."

"Lay it on me." Regina laughed, trying to break the tension.

Charlotte did not smile. "I think," she began, "that I need a little time away from my parents. Every time I call them I'm getting long, stony silences on the phone. I think either they're sick with worry about what's going to happen to me, or they're just mad at me, which is more likely."

Regina nodded. "Yeah."

"But anyway, it will most likely take a while for things to go back to normal with them. So a little distance may be in order."

"Go on…"

"I like my job at USD. I can work on my dissertation. I get to read and study at my desk. And," she said, grinning, "I have interlibrary loan privilege."

"That reminds me," Regina said. "Tell Marty you want your stuff back. The Feds should let you go to the evidence warehouse and retrieve it."

"Is that why you asked me to put those books in my suitcase? So I can get them back?"

Regina made a dismissive gesture. "More like so they wouldn't get scattered in the shuffle. By the way, I've been paying some overdue book fines."

"I'll get them as soon as we arrive back. Thank you."

"No problem."

Charlotte took Regina's hand. "I want to stay. With three conditions."

Regina attempted to keep a poker face. She wasn't successful. "Just three?"

"First: I pay rent. I've been freeloading off you long enough. Don't even argue."

Regina shrugged. "Not necessary, but if that's what you want, fine. What's the second thing?"

"You understand that I could leave. I might go back to Wisconsin. Who knows, I might just get on a plane and go to Israel."

Regina did a double take. "You're Jewish?"

"I'm thinking of converting."

"With a name like Charlotte Hammarskjold?"

"Yeah. So?"

"O-kay. What's the third thing?"

"I move out of that goddamned living room and sleep in your bed. Because, honestly," Charlotte sighed, "I don't think I can take another night on that couch. It hurts my back."

"Really." Regina lifted an eyebrow. "Is THAT the reason you want to share my bed?"

"Of course."

"Uh-huh."

Regina placed her hand on Charlotte's knee. Charlotte did not move. Regina's hand traveled up, slowly, sliding under Charlotte's pretty sundress.

A deep flush crept up Charlotte's neck, up her face, and disappeared inside her blonde hair.

"Oh my," Regina said. "Sure you just want to sleep with me for my mattress?"

Charlotte shifted, letting Regina's hand slip higher. "So, what do you say?"

"To what?" Regina's breathing had become labored.

"To my conditions, silly."

"I accept."

"Good…"

The rest of Charlotte's sentence was cut off by Regina's deep hungry kiss.

When she finally pulled away, Charlotte opened her eyes. "Wow."

Regina grinned. "Close the curtains."

Charlotte stood up, obeying. When she turned from the window, she saw Regina flipping the wall light switch. The room darkened.

They approached each other. Regina brushed blonde hair from Charlotte's face.

"You don't know how long I have dreamt about this," Regina whispered.

Charlotte smiled. "I think I have a pretty good idea."

Regina began kissing her. She went slow, letting things build.

Charlotte placed her hands on Regina's hips, pressing her fingers.

Regina began to kiss Charlotte's face, pausing to nibble her earlobe.

"Feels nice," Charlotte said for lack of anything else. She seemed suddenly shy.

Straightening, Regina looked into Charlotte's eyes and smiled. Then she began unbuttoning the sundress's collar.

"Those buttons are tricky," Charlotte said. Her voice sounded high and nervous. "I bought this in a thrift store. You probably know the one, it's down the street from your house and around the corner from the supermarket…"

Regina had freed the last button. She gently raised Charlotte's arms high.

"…And this was the only dress in my size," Charlotte continued in her same high-pitched tone, as if nothing at all was happening. "I thought it looked a little old-lady-ish, but then I thought, I guess it's better than nothing…"

Regina bent at the waist and lifted Charlotte's dress up and off of her in a fluid movement. In her underwear with her hands up, Charlotte looked like the comic victim of a stickup artist who had stolen her clothes.

"…So I bought it anyway. I don't know. Do you like it?"

"Your dress?" Regina kissed Charlotte's neck.

The blonde gasped. "I don't remember what it looks like." Regina snuggled in close, sliding her arms around the other girl's back to unfasten her bra.

"That's, uh, a shame," Charlotte stuttered.

Regina tossed the bra onto the cot with a flick of her wrist. "It certainly is," she breathed. Kneeling on the floor, Regina pulled Charlotte's white cottons down slowly, staring unblinking at the thatch of blonde pubic hair that was revealed inch by inch. Sliding her arms around Charlotte's thighs as if embracing a lover, she buried her face into the blonde bush.

"Oh God," Charlotte gasped. She closed her eyes and teetered. Then she began to fall, toppling like a tree.

Regina let go only barely in time. Charlotte twisted in mid-fall and caught herself on one of the bedposts. Her feet skidded across the floor as she struggled to right herself.

"Sorry," Regina said.

"Quite all right," Charlotte said after a gasp.

Regina gave her a saucy glance. She then walked to the four-poster and stripped naked in ten seconds flat before hopping up onto the bed, to the pillows. Her firm, tight body was lithe and strong.

Reaching the headboard, she flipped over, sat up, and smiled.

Charlotte smiled back.

Inwardly, however, she was panicking.

Charlotte felt attracted to Regina. Ever since that magical moment in the car with that kiss (those TWO kisses), the Wisconsin girl had been enamored of Regina. She had been ready to sleep with her the first night at Regina's house, and had been disappointed when her host had unexpectedly said no. Charlotte had later flirted and teased. She had thought she was ready.

Now, however, at the crucial moment—now that it was ACTUALLY HAPPENING—there was no denying it.

Charlotte was absolutely terrified.

Relax, she told herself. *Slow your heart down. It's going to be fine.*

Regina looked Charlotte up and down. "Curvy girl."

Charlotte tried to smile. "That's what they tell me."

"That's what your mirror tells you. God, you are a sexy, sexy woman." Regina paused. She saw the hesitation in Charlotte's eyes.

Relax, Charlotte repeated to herself. But she felt frozen.

Regina's body language changed. She shifted from her come-hither pose and turned onto her side, propping her head up on her arm in an easy-going manner. "So, I was going to tell you about the seafood restaurant next door."

"Yeah?"

"It's really funky. I bet some hippies own it. I wonder if they catch their own fish…"

As Regina made relaxed conversation, she eased herself off the bed and gently approached Charlotte, taking her hand. Slowly, Regina led Charlotte by the hand up onto the bed. As the blonde crawled up with Regina toward the pillows, her big boobs wobbled over the comforter.

"Maybe we can eat dinner there tonight, if you want," Regina said. She flopped back down, smiling, on her side.

"Yeah, sure," Charlotte said. She lowered herself onto her side facing Regina, as awkward and nervous as a girl on her first date.

"Not sure we should eat any seafood though," Regina said. She brushed Charlotte's blonde hair over her ear. "You know what they say."

"What's that?"

"It's a proven fact that most people who eat good seafood live longer. And most people who eat bad seafood are ready to die."

Charlotte laughed at the corny joke, releasing tension.

Regina kept talking. After a while, she and Charlotte settled into what had now become an old routine: talking, teasing, laughing. Regina kept stroking Charlotte's hair. Every now and then, she would lean over and kiss her gently.

Finally, Regina stopped talking and just kissed Charlotte. The brunette went slowly, sliding her mouth over hers, feeling the tiny ridges in her lips.

Charlotte accepted the kisses passively. But she did not feel panicked, like before. *This is okay,* she thought. And then: *it's better than okay.*

Regina shifted her body closer, wiggling in tight. Charlotte lifted her arm to make room, draping it over the other woman's neck.

Regina touched Charlotte's lips with her tongue; Charlotte opened her mouth. They began to make out. Regina slid her hand up and down Charlotte's back, slipping her fingers now and then through the Wisconsin girl's luxurious long blonde hair.

So gentle, Charlotte thought. She began to feel heat rising in her body.

Regina shifted again, slipping her knee through Charlotte's thighs. The blonde's body was damp with sweat. Charlotte gasped. Regina pushed her gently onto her back.

Charlotte opened her eyes. Regina was kissing down her chest. Then she paused.

"Scoot up," she whispered.

Charlotte obeyed, digging her elbows into the bed to prop her body up on the pillows.

Adjusting, Regina gained leverage and scissored her legs, rubbing her vulva upon her lover's with a slow steady rolling of her hips.

Charlotte's jaw dropped. She felt her own wetness as Regina slid her pubic mound upon Charlotte's, up and down, up and down, in a rich slow rhythm.

Regina's lips traced a languorous line up

Charlotte's breast, climbing, until her mouth just touched the edge of the pink aureole. Moaning, she dragged her tongue over Charlotte's nipple over and over again, taking her time, licking the nipple into hardness.

"Wow," Charlotte heard herself say. She looked down. Regina's eyes were closed as she licked and sucked the big breasts, moving from one to the other. Charlotte reached and cradled Regina's head with tenderness, running her fingers through the buzz-cut hair.

Regina shifted her hips, moving lower. She kissed down Charlotte's stomach.

Charlotte looked up at the ceiling. She reached with her hand and found Regina's hand. Their fingers interlaced, squeezing tight.

Regina slid her body down still lower, gazing at the silky golden triangle. "Oh, honey," she said in a husky voice. "I've wanted you so long."

Charlotte turned her face to the side, closed her eyes, and squeezed Regina's hand harder.

Regina kissed the sodden bush very gently, letting her lips linger. Charlotte inhaled. Shifting once more, Regina moved her mouth around Charlotte's wet warm slit, tasting and inhaling the beautiful woman.

"Honey," Regina repeated, as if in a trance. Then, using her lips, she parted the blonde curls to place the lightest of kisses upon the top of Charlotte's opening.

The blonde girl heard moaning. She finally

realized the sound was coming from within her. And then, when she did, she realized that she could not stop, that it was expressing a place deep down inside of her that had never been tapped before.

Charlotte's eyes snapped open. She looked down. Regina was eating her. *It's so good,* Charlotte thought. Her hips began moving involuntarily, a slow belly-dancer's roll. Regina moved with her, not missing a beat.

Writhing, Charlotte caught her reflection in the big antique mirror across the room. It was an impossibly erotic scene: a blonde, voluptuous naked girl in a big four-poster bed like out of a romance novel, with her lover between her legs, bringing her to climax. Charlotte wondered for a split-second if Regina had wanted it this way, if Regina had known that this would be their first time and had wanted to make it special. *Thank you Regina.*

The orgasm hit Charlotte with a force she had never before experienced, shaking her body and making her scream. Finally she gasped, almost sobbing, before pulling Regina up.

Regina lay gently on top of her. She kissed the tears away from her face.

With an abrupt jerk, Regina stopped. She raised her body up.

Charlotte opened her eyes. "Huh?"

"What did you say?"

"Nothing."

"Yes, you did." Regina studied her. Her eyes looked odd. "You said, 'I love you.'"

"No I didn't."

"YES YOU DID."

Stunned, Charlotte realized it was true: the words had escaped from her, lower than a whisper, almost a sigh. *I did not think those words,* Charlotte thought. *I do not know where those words came from.*

Regina continued to hold her body up and stare. She seemed ready to stay there all night.

Charlotte swallowed. "Yes, I said it."

"Is it true?"

An eternity passed. Charlotte knew that if she said yes, she was locked in: whatever she and Regina did in bed from now on would mean something. It wasn't a fling.

Suddenly, Charlotte realized where the real fear was coming from: a fear of hurting Regina, the person she had come to trust more than anyone in the world, the person who perhaps cared for her even more than her own family. *If I ever hurt Regina,* Charlotte thought, *I would never forgive myself.*

And then, a split-second later, she decided to stop being afraid.

"Yes," Charlotte said. "I love you."

Regina kept staring, skeptical, as if Charlotte was trying to sell her a vacuum cleaner at her door. "Say it again."

"I love you."

"Say it again."

"I love yoooouuuuuu…"

Regina screamed and hugged Charlotte so hard the blonde coughed.

"Oh my God!" Regina said. She started to cry. "I love YOU. But you guessed that already. Right?"

"Not really," Charlotte said. She groaned, rubbing her clavicle.

"I can't believe it." Regina looked at her lover with wonder. "It's…okay, I was going to make a smart-aleck joke like I usually do, but that doesn't feel right. So…thank you."

"I love you." Charlotte smiled.

Regina's face broke into a goofy grin that she possibly had never, ever made before.

"You're so cute," Charlotte said. She touched her face. "I mean that, you know?"

"I've been called a lot of things, but never cute. So, thank you again."

They kissed for a while, stroking each other's hair, listening to the distant waves.

After a time, Charlotte shifted her body, kissing down. She lingered at Regina's small breasts, staring and rubbing them tenderly, as if they were precious things. Opening her mouth, she gently licked a small raspberry-colored nipple.

"Aaaahhhh," Regina said, as if stepping into a wonderfully hot bath. She smiled, eyes closed, and stretched like a cat.

Charlotte kissed all around the breast peaks, going slowly, feeling the soft firm flesh of her lips. Tentatively, she slid her hand down further. Regina gently lifted her knee up into the side, inviting the touch.

Charlotte raised her head and giggled nervously. "Is there a manual?"

Regina played with Charlotte's long blonde hair, sliding her fingers through the locks. "No, I already checked interlibrary loan. Sorry."

"Damn." Charlotte's shaky fingers had reached the boundary of Regina's pubic area. Regina arched her hips gently, sliding her mons under Charlotte's fingers. Charlotte felt Regina's heat. After a moment of hesitation, Charlotte turned on her side, moving her head and shoulders down, facing away from her lover. Regina betrayed an expression of nervousness and impatience, biting her lip hard. But she placed an easy hand on Charlotte's back, rubbing.

"Wow," Charlotte breathed. She stared down at Regina's neatly-trimmed bush, inches from her face. Touching the slit with her finger, Charlotte's jaw dropped as she saw a bead of moisture appear inside the thin brown forest.

"God, sweetie," Regina whispered. "I don't want to be pushy. I don't want to rush you. But…can you just please give me one kiss…please?"

Charlotte kept staring, motionless. After a long time had passed, she brushed her long blonde hair from her face, lowered it, and pressed her lips against Regina's soft wet mound.

Regina moaned. Her head sank back deep into her pillow as her eyes rolled up and her lids closed. "It's so good, honey," she whispered. "Oh, Charlotte. So good. With you…"

Charlotte kissed again, letting her lips linger, feeling the scratchy stubble of Regina's trimmed hair. Regina made no sound, but Charlotte felt Regina's body begin vibrating, radiating hunger. She felt Regina's need.

"I'm nervous," Charlotte whispered, so softly Regina almost did not hear.

"Don't be," Regina said. She breathed harder. "God, honey, I want…you. Let go. LET GO."

Closing her eyes, Charlotte lowered her face once more, opening her mouth this time. Her tongue found Regina's clitoris immediately, swollen and thrusting up like an angry hot pebble. Charlotte began sliding the tip of her tongue over the angry organ, feeling the slippery wetness of Regina, tasting her. Charlotte moaned.

With a violent jerk, Regina wailed. Charlotte lifted her head, startled.

The blonde girl studied her lover. Regina was covered in tiny drops of sweat, hyperventilating. At length she opened her eyes and saw Charlotte's face over hers once more.

"Was that…" Charlotte began, faltering.

"Yes. Oh, yes," Regina gasped.

"Did I go too fast?"

The brunette laughed, sliding her fingers through her buzz cut. She raised her face to kiss

Charlotte's lips. "No. Not at all."

"Okay." Charlotte smiled.

"Better than okay."

"Yeah, I kind of figured."

Regina gave her a sour look. Then she touched her own damp face, wiping her eyes.

"I guess we need to go to dinner soon, huh?" Charlotte asked in a voice that did not sound enthusiastic.

"I'm sure the place is open late. We can stay here a little while longer."

Charlotte smiled and kissed Regina again. "Cool."

Many hours passed. Secrets were told, promises made, mountains moved.

Finally, Regina yawned. She glanced at the window. No light at all came through the curtain. "It's late. Maybe we're not having dinner after all."

"That's okay," Charlotte giggled. "I'm not hungry."

"For food, anyway."

"Bitch."

"That's what they call me."

"We can have an extra big breakfast."

"Yeah."

They held each other, spooning under the covers. Charlotte heard the ocean through the window. She felt drowsy. As her eyes closed, she smiled at the thought of many more days and nights with Regina.

As sleep took her, she wondered in her academic mind, *how ironic*. It was only through the most terrible time of her life with a drug dealer that, she, Charlotte, had discovered the greatest drug of all.

The End

Thanks for reading! If you have time, please review *The 420 Uh-Oh*. I read every review, and I appreciate honest feedback!

If you enjoyed this book, you may also enjoy

The Beard

By Anne Eton

When tall, pretty Kelly interviews at Washington D.C.'s premier LGBT-centric lobbying firm, she claims she has a girlfriend. Nothing could be further from the truth; she's never even kissed a girl. Kelly's hired. However, a suspicious co-worker keeps inquiring about her girlfriend. To keep her lies straight, Kelly bases her fictional partner on Anna, an aggressive, gorgeous lesbian friend of a friend. But when the firm's annual Christmas party looms, Kelly's forced to produce her mysterious girlfriend. The real Anna agrees to be Kelly's "beard"—her fake date. But at the party, alcohol flows… and Anna's all over Kelly. Kelly pretends to her office mates that her "girlfriend's" advances are perfectly normal—even as she feels her resistance to the beautiful woman melting away.

The Beard is a comedy with sexy scenes and some explicit passages.

Excerpt follows!

The Beard

Excerpt:

Kelly stumbled, tipsy. Anna guided her with a sure hand to the office supply room, opening the door and escorting her inside.

"Hey! Office supplies," Kelly said with false cheer. She looked around nervously. "You need some gel pens? Ha, ha!"

Anna smirked. She shut the door behind them and pressed the doorknob's button, locking it.

"Or paper clips, or toner," Kelly babbled, casually backing away. "It's a regular Staples in here!"

"Yes," Anna replied. The blonde gave Anna a sexy look and flipped a wall switch. The room went dark.

"I think we should talk about expectations," Kelly said in the pitch black, as if discussing the price of a car. "I admit, I did sort of use you for my own ends…"

"Yes."

Kelly felt Anna's hands. The tall girl backed away; she came up against waist-high pallets of paper boxes.

"You see," Kelly gasped, "I know we're supposed to be pretending that you're my girlfriend—"

"Yes… yes…" Anna murmured. She began slipping Kelly's dress up as the taller girl moved awkwardly against the immovable cartons.

Also by Anne Eton

ABOUT THE AUTHOR

I write first-time F/F erotic romance. I love what I do!

If you would like to know when I publish new books, please sign up for my New Release Mailing List, at my site! I don't share my readers' email with anyone, for any reason.

www.anneeton.com

Thanks for reading!

Anne

www.ingramcontent.com/pod-product-compliance
Lightning Source LLC
Chambersburg PA
CBHW071314200626
46813CB00015B/2206